Redeeming Your Home

by Jeanette Strauss

Please note that the name "satan" and all names related to him are not capitalized. I have made a conscious decision not to capitalize his name, even to the point of violating grammar rules.

Publisher: Glorious Creations 2016 www.gloriouscreations.net

Table of Contents

Foreword

Redeeming Your Home was written in response to requests from people who have read my book *From God's Hands to Your Land.* They have redeemed their land and experienced significant, positive results, and have asked for information on cleansing their homes and businesses.

The original plan was to add details concerning spiritually cleansing a home into the *Land* book. Because of the amount of information that needed to be addressed, it became apparent that adding a chapter or two wouldn't adequately cover the subject.

This book contains my personal testimony of how the Lord led my husband and me into this ministry, and it contains testimonies from others who have received positive, life changing results from spiritually cleansing their home, There is a testimony where cleansing and dedicating a person's home may have saved a life!

I personally believe that this is a spiritual field that is waiting to be harvested. I believe the Lord is saying, "Take notice, this field is ripe for harvest — go forth and set my people free!" (John 4:35)

Some have used their testimony of ridding their homes and land of demons as a means of leading someone to Christ. We have witnessed how this scriptural method of cleansing land and homes has inspired people and given them the knowledge to help others. When they see and experience the reality of how this really works, they want to get into their Bibles to learn more. This is a way to change a neighborhood, and even a city.

Finally, my brethren, be strong in the Lord and in the power of His might. Put on the whole armor of God, that you may be able to stand against the wiles of the devil. For we do not wrestle against flesh and blood, but against principalities, against powers, against the rulers of the darkness of this age, against spiritual hosts of wickedness in the heavenly places.

~ Ephesians 6:10-13

Chapter 1

Unexplained Activity

Over the years, we have experienced that there are evil spirits whose jobs are to cause as many problems as they can for people, especially in their homes. As you read my story and the experiences of others, I hope you will be encouraged and inspired to spiritually cleanse and dedicate your home or apartment to the Lord. I have learned that many people share a testimony like ours that consists of having mysterious occurrences or happenings in their homes with no reasonable, physical explanation.

The problems I am talking about may include sounds, voices, doors slamming, or someone or something walking around. If there are children in the house, they may complain they are afraid that someone is watching them as they are trying to go to sleep, or that they see things or people in the house. When you investigate, there is nothing you can find that accounts for their fears.

I realize we can't pin everything on demon infestation. However, I have learned that, as a Christian, when you do a spiritual house cleansing and dedicate your home to the Lord Jesus Christ, most often the unexplained sounds and activity ceases.

For those who haven't had any of the experiences that are shared in this book, you may know someone who is struggling with unexplained, negative activity in their home. I hope that after reading this book you will be better equipped to help them and their home get set free.

Introduction to the spirit world

When my husband and I first became born again believers, our spiritual eyes were opened as never before. We had gone to church as children and grown up believing in Jesus, but neither one of us had what we considered a personal relationship with Him. That is, until we moved to Florida and got involved with a non-denominational spirit-filled church. At that time, we really became "born again" believers. We had a real life change, and developed a personal relationship with Jesus.

We hadn't heard much about the baptism of the Holy Spirit until then. After studying about this gift in the Bible, we prayed to the Lord and asked Him to baptize us with His Holy Spirit and give us all of the gifts listed in 1 Corinthians 12, including the gift of speaking in other tongues. After receiving this gift of praying in other tongues, we began asking the Lord to take us deeper in our walk with the Holy Spirit.

During our prayer times, we would begin by praying in English, then switch over and pray in the Spirit. We ended our prayers in this way to insure that we didn't miss anything the Holy Spirit wanted included in our prayers.

In my book, *From the Courtroom of Heaven to the Throne Room of Grace and Mercy* there is a chapter about receiving the baptism in the Holy Spirit. You will find this chapter to be helpful if you haven't received this gift from the Lord and would like to. You can also read about this experience in Acts 2:2-4. This baptism of the Holy Spirit gives us power to overcome our enemies.

Jesus was empowered by the Holy Spirit, and we should we, if we want to do the things He did.

> *How God anointed Jesus of Nazareth with the Holy Ghost and with power, who went about doing good, and healing all that were oppressed with the devil, for God was with him.*
> *~ Acts 10:38*

We discovered that, as believers, the Bible says we become citizens of the Kingdom of God. We physically live on the earth, but spiritually we have access to all of the benefits of living in God's spiritual kingdom. This equips us to live a life of victory while we are living on the earth.

An example of one of the benefits of the Kingdom of God would be the armor of God spoken of in Ephesians 6. This is spiritual armor, but we need it because we are daily fighting spiritual battles in this physical realm.

> *Finally, my brethren, be strong in the Lord and in the power of His might. Put on the whole armor of God, that you may be able to stand against the wiles of the devil. For we do not wrestle against flesh and blood, but against principalities, against powers, against the rulers of the darkness of this age, against*

spiritual hosts of wickedness in the heavenly places. ~ Ephesians 6:10-13

We learned that one of the differences between living as citizens in the physical realm, and having access spiritually as citizens of the Kingdom of God, was an awakening to the spiritual forces that are active here on the earth. This includes both good forces called angels, and evil ones called demons.

We learned about the precious blood of Jesus and what a powerful weapon it is in our spiritual battles. As a new believer, a person can be compared to a soldier in boot camp who has been placed in the midst of a battle in need of proper training. Without the help and power of the Holy Spirit and the gifts of the Spirit (1 Corinthians12:1-11), life on earth would be very difficult to navigate.

One of the first spiritual battles we encountered and were very unprepared for, was that our new home had others inhabiting it besides ourselves. They came with the house and they were spiritual in nature and evil.

Chapter 2

Evil Spirits Living in Our Home

One night shortly after moving into our home in Florida, I was awakened by sounds coming from our kitchen. I could hear people laughing on the other side of the bedroom door that opened into the kitchen. I heard glasses clinking, voices talking, and could smell cigarette smoke. From the conversation I heard, it sounded like they were playing some kind of a card game. I heard a chair scraping on the floor as if someone was sliding back from the table to get up.

I glanced at the clock and saw that it was 2:00 am. Deciding not to wake my husband before investigating a little on my own, I quietly got out of bed and walked over to the door to listen. I could still hear the talking and laughing. I opened the door a crack to take a peek and looked into the kitchen. The kitchen was bathed in a soft light from a street light outside, but no one was there. I thought I must have been wrong about hearing and smelling things, so I went back to bed.

About an hour later, I was awakened by the same sounds. I laid there for several minutes to make sure I was really hearing the noises. It sounded like a party was going on. I got up again and looked—but no one was there.

I don't remember why I didn't wake my husband, but I may have been concerned that he would make a noise if I roused him and the noises would stop. It was unusual for me not to wake him up because that would be my natural inclination. If I hear a noise at night in the house I am quick to wake him up and say; "Bud! I hear a noise; would you get up and check it out?"

That night I didn't wake him up. I went back to bed and began to pray. I asked the Lord what it was, and the Holy Spirit answered and said that it was "a party spirit." I had never heard of such a thing. In fact, the only spirit I knew about at that time was the Holy Spirit. After praying for a while I fell back to sleep and slept through the night.

The next morning I told Bud about the noises, and he suggested we ask someone at the church if they had heard anything like this happening. It would be several days until we would be going back to church.

But the next morning I was watching The 700 Club and heard a woman giving her testimony. She shared that while on vacation, she and her husband had stopped for the night at a hotel. The door to their room opened to the poolside.

She woke up about 2:00 a.m. to the sounds of a party going on outside their door. She could hear people in the pool yelling and laughing. She could hear the sounds of people walking past their room, talking and laughing.

She called the manager to complain. He told her the pool had closed down at 10:00 p.m. so no one should be in it, but said he would send someone right over to check. She went to the door and opened it and no one was there.

She called the manager back and told him it must have been someone in an adjoining room who had their TV on too loud.

She went back to sleep thinking that was it. However, a short time later she woke up again to the same sounds. She got out of bed and opened the door; she looked but no one was there. When she went back to bed, she asked the Lord what this was. He told her it was a "party spirit." What an amazing coincidence!

Pat Robertson explained how any building, including a person's home, could have spirits residing in them. This is especially true if the people who have lived in the home, or others who had come in for visits, had spirits attached to them. Those spirits see something in the house that attracts them and they stay. It's also possible that the people who live in the home possess certain items that attract evil spirits.

He shared that houses can have spirits still residing in them from previous tenants. He went on to encourage people to pray through their home and perform a spiritual housecleaning to make sure their home is free of any demonic influences that can cause problems.

He explained that to spiritually cleanse a home, a person walks through their home room-by-room, praying and asking the Lord if there is anything in the room that isn't pleasing to Him or that might have a demonic spirit attached to it. He said that demons don't like Christians because the presence of the Lord is always with them and evil spirits don't like to be in God's presence.

I later learned that when a Christian moves into a home inhabited by demons, the demons won't leave on their own; they have to be driven out. The demon's goal is to get the people out of the home so they can have control over it. Usually the spirits will try different things to scare the people who live in the home so they will move out.

Demons in a home are capable of almost anything. We have witnessed threatening manifestations and heard testimonies of the different ways they operate. People can lose the battle because they don't understand what is going on, and they give in and sell the house to the next unsuspecting family.

We shared our experience with our pastor. He instructed us to pray a prayer of repentance on behalf of any sin that may have been committed in our home by us or by any previous tenants, and to ask forgiveness for the sin. By doing this, we would remove any spiritual legal rights the demons had to stay there.

So we did this. We began by praying to the Lord for wisdom, and asked Him to reveal anything in our home that wasn't pleasing to him. We walked through each room looking at each item, praying for insight that would show us if a demon might be attached to it. We couldn't find anything. We decided that this particular problem had come with the house from previous owners.

We anointed the doorposts and window frames with olive oil. We commanded any demons to go, especially any party spirits that might be there. We asked the Lord to cleanse and cover our home with the blood of Jesus. We ended by declaring that any spiritual doors or windows that had been open to the enemy and had allowed him to come into our home were now closed to him permanently.

After praying, we decreed that our home belonged to the Lord and was dedicated to His service and would be used to fulfill His purposes.

The 'party spirit' left and never returned. Later, we found out that the previous owners lived in the house six months out of the year. They owned greyhounds that they raced at the local dog track during the winter months. That in itself might not be bad, but there can be a kind of lifestyle attached to this type of job that could have invited the party spirit, although it could have come from any previous owners.

Our testimony of being able to help others

In the meantime, as we shared our testimony with others, we found more information on the need to cleanse our homes.

We discovered that ours wasn't an isolated case. Other people were having problems in their homes, and we had an opportunity to pray with them. We walked with them through each room, praying with them and removing objects as the Holy Spirit quickened us. Each time, we did this we increased in knowledge in this particular area of ministry. We collected many testimonies to the goodness of God and the power of His blood.

As time went on we, began to have an under-standing that some of the problems people have in their homes were rooted to the land under the house. Some people live on property where something traumatic has happened on the land. Maybe blood had been shed or, at one time, there had been an altar to satan in that location.

Either of these would provide a legal right for any curses to operate, until a believer prays a prayer of intercession on behalf of the sin committed and breaks the curse off the land and any buildings sitting on it.

> *Lest innocent blood be shed in your land, which the Lord your God gives you as an inheritance, and so blood guilt be upon you.*
> *~ Deuteronomy 19:10*

Since demons come with a curse, negative repercussions can come to the people living on the property.

A curse with frightening results

Here is an instance of the haunting of a home where there had been bloodshed committed on the land, and a curse was affecting the person in the house.

We received a call from a woman who told us that her oldest son had just turned 16. Since his birthday a few days earlier, he was being attacked every night by something. They didn't know what it was, but they thought the "thing" was a spirit. The physical attacks against him were growing more violent each night and he was afraid to sleep in his room. His mother was afraid that it was going to kill him.

She said she and her mother (who lived with them) were Christians, but the son who was having the problems wasn't. There were two younger children living in the home who weren't having any problems like the oldest son. Their story was bizarre.

On the evening of the day her son had turned 16, he was lying on his bed watching TV. A picture of a western landscape that showed a prairie and a buffalo herd was on the wall next to the TV. That night, he noticed a movement out of the corner of his eye and looked over at the picture. Suddenly it was as if the buffalos were stampeding out of the picture toward him. He felt something physically jump on him and choke him. He fought to get free. He finally got loose and ran down stairs. It didn't follow him, but he was afraid to go back up to his room that night, and slept on the floor in his mom's room.

The next day he was taking a nap in his room. He thought that maybe he had imagined the attack. Suddenly a loud sound woke him up. His TV had fallen out of the entertainment center and crashed to the floor.

Once again, something jumped on him and began to choke him. He had a harder time getting away than the first time, but he managed to run down the stairs to tell his mom what had happened. She went upstairs and the TV was lying on the floor. There was no visible reason for it to have fallen out of the entertainment center.

That night the grandmother prayed and asked the Lord to show her what was happening, and why this spirit was attacking her grandson. A man appeared to her in a dream. She asked him what he was doing there. The man spoke to her and said that he had a 16-year-old son who had been killed on that property by an Indian. He had come to revenge the death of his son. He told her that her grandson was an Indian and he had just turned 16, so he was justified—blood for blood. Then the man disappeared.

The same night the grandmother had the dream, the young man was attacked again as he was sleeping on the couch. Everyone else had gone to bed and he was alone in the living room. He said he was awakened by someone jumping on him and choking him.

He got free and slept in his mom's room again and was left alone. The next morning the mom called us and asked us to please come over and pray with them.

Bud and I went over to their house. They told us the story, and the grandmother shared her dream. We asked if the Indian claim was true, because none of the children looked like Native Americans, especially the 16 year old. He was blonde haired and blue eyed.

The mother explained that the young man's grandmother (on his father's side) was a full blood Native American who had married a white man. The visitor in the dream had been telling the truth about that, even though it was a familiar spirit and not the actual father of the boy who had been killed. The spirit had found a legal right in the spirit realm and really did want to kill the young man. Could it have killed him? I don't know, only the Lord knows how far the enemy can carry things in the physical realm, especially if he finds a legal way in.

We explained to the young man that Jesus was the only one who could stop the attack. Only believers had the right and authority to use the name of Jesus to stop this spirit from its mission. We told him a story from the Bible about this very thing. We explained that there were some men who had seen the disciples of Jesus cast demons or evil spirits out of people, using the name of Jesus. These particular men weren't believers themselves, but they witnessed the power over the demons the believers had when they used the name of Jesus to cast out demons. They decided they wanted to try it on a man who had a demon in him. They attempted to use the authority in the name of Jesus to cast out the evil spirit in a man. The spirit came out of the man and attacked them.

Then some of the itinerant Jewish exorcists took it upon themselves to call the name of the Lord Jesus over those who had evil spirits, saying, "We exorcise you by the Jesus whom Paul preaches." And the evil spirit answered and said, "Jesus I know, and Paul I know; but who are you?" Then the man in whom the evil spirit was leaped on them, overpowered them, and prevailed against them, so that they fled out of that house naked and wounded. This became known both to all Jews and Greeks dwelling in Ephesus; and fear fell on them all, and the name of the Lord Jesus was magnified. And many who had believed came confessing and telling their deeds. ~ Acts 19:13-25

After sharing the story with him, we explained that what was happening to him was the work of an evil spirit connected to the land and the house because of the bloodshed that had happened here. The only way to guarantee the eviction of this spirit from his life was if he made a commitment to Jesus Christ as His Savior. We shared that Jesus had a plan for his life, and this experience would prove to him the power that Jesus has over the devil. We told him that he would need to pray and confess that he believed that Jesus Christ was the son of God who had come to earth to save him. He would need to repent for his sins and ask forgiveness for them and ask Jesus to come into his life.

He was familiar with Jesus because of his mother and grandmother's influence, but he had never made a personal commitment. We told him that the decision was a free choice. He thought about it and said that he wanted to know that he belonged to Jesus, so we prayed the salvation prayer with him.

Then we prayed over the situation. The mom prayed a prayer of repentance on behalf of the sin committed against the boy who had been killed by the Native American Indian, asking for the Lord's forgiveness. We prayed a prayer for sin committed in the generational bloodline that could affect the children in the house, and asked forgiveness for the sin. We asked the Lord to remove the familiar spirit and block it from any further attack against the family. (More information about this type of prayer is found in my book *From the Courtroom of Heaven to the Throne Room of Grace and Mercy — Prayers and Petitions.*)

We then walked through the house, going room-to-room, praying and anointing every door and windowsill. When we entered the room of the young man, we felt a cold presence. It felt like death as we prayed. More than one of us felt it immediately. We spent extra time in that room, repenting for any sin committed in it that would welcome a spirit of death into the house. We finally felt it lift and go. None of the other bedrooms had that feeling.

As we came downstairs and started to go through the rooms, the mother shared that over the years she and others had seen a little girl ghost. She hadn't given it much thought because it hadn't caused any problems. When anything was moved around, or they heard a weird sound, or at times they would notice the dog would seem to be staring at something, they would joke and say it was the little girl again. She said they just thought about it as an innocent house guest. After the prayer, the little girl never showed up again. I know there are people who have this type of house guest that seem innocent and a novelty, but they aren't innocent. They could open the door for trouble. We finished our spiritual housecleaning prayer and a prayer for the land and we left. The mother said she would let us know about any changes.

We spoke with her several days later and she said the attacks against her son stopped immediately. She told us she had spoken with a neighbor who was in her late 80's and had lived in the neighborhood all of her life. She asked her if she knew if anyone had ever died in her house (the house we prayed through). The neighbor said that a man had died in an upstairs bedroom. She couldn't remember how or why he died.

The need for spiritual housecleaning

Spiritual housecleaning is as necessary and valid today as it was in Bible days. One of the best examples of spiritually cleansing a house and removing items that can cause trouble in your life is found in the New Testament.

> ...many that believed came and confessed and showed their deeds. Many of them also which used curious arts brought their books together, and burned them before all men, and they counted the price of them, and found it to be fifty thousand pieces of silver. ~ Acts 19:18-19

This scripture confirms that as people became "born again" believers in Jesus, they went through their homes and removed any objects that connected them to their old lives, items tied in any way to the worship of foreign gods. They understood that they needed to rid their homes and lives of such objects and all that came with them. The objects had the potential to affect their new spiritual walk in a negative way. The scripture says they burned the items openly, in front of their neighbors and friends, as a testimony. By burning the items, they were making sure that no one else would be able to read the books or use the cursed objects in any way.

It would certainly have an impact on those who watched as to how serious the new converts were about turning their back on their old ways, as they embraced their new faith. They didn't want anything left in their homes that might bind them to their past life.

These books and scrolls full of magic charms, amulets and incantations were well known in Ephesus and they were very valuable.

... be self- controlled and alert your enemy the devil prowls around like a roaring lion looking for someone to devour.

~ 1 Peter 5:8 NIV

Chapter 3

What Needs To Be Removed?

There are negative repercussions when you have something in your home that the Lord clearly hates and says in His Word not to have. Some believers live their lives not thinking about the connection between negative spiritual roots that are attached to their possessions, and what is happening in their lives.

As a Christian, if you have any of these items in your home and do not eliminate them, there will be spiritual consequences. These consequences can and will develop into physical penalties for you or those living in the house, if left unchecked.

The accuser of the brethren (satan) is alive and well and he hates believers. He is sly and crafty, and works in various ways to attack Christians. As believers, we are warned in the Bible to be spiritually alert.

> ... be self- controlled and alert your enemy the
> devil prowls around like a roaring lion looking
> for someone to devour. ~ 1 Peter 5:8 NIV

Jesus loves us and has plans and purposes for us. He doesn't want us to remain ignorant of satan's schemes that are specially fashioned to lead us off track.

Once a person becomes a believer in Jesus Christ, the Kingdom of Light that is now within him will clash with the kingdom of darkness that is evicted from him. When we become born again, our spirits are renewed and become new. Our soul nature, which is our mind, will and emotions, takes a little longer to wash clean.

A new believer may feel there is something that isn't right, but there is nothing specific they can pin that feeling on. It seems like something is working against them, and there surely might be. Bad things can and do happen to believers, and that's life on earth. The various trials a believer goes through can be used as a testimony to the glory of the Lord—after we get through them. However, some trials can be avoided by being spiritually attentive.

What does the Lord hate?

In general, unless a person had been involved in witchcraft before becoming a Christian, they would have no reason to sharpen their spiritual senses to pay attention to what they had in their homes that could keep the door to their past open to demonic activity.

There are items that are a direct connection to the kingdom of darkness. Some of these items would include Ouija boards, tarot cards, horoscope, and astrology study. They are not innocent items for children or adults to play with, as many have been led to believe. They are tools used by satan to entice people to communicate with demons. These practices will open the door to demonic activity into one's life.

Consulting a medium is prohibited

I have heard stories of people who were so desperate to rid their home of what might be demonic spiritual activity, they asked the advice of those who call themselves mediums, psychics, spiritual counselors or demonologists, thinking they would find out why the spirits were there and how to get rid of them.

According to the Bible, these mediums are agents themselves, representatives of the kingdom of darkness. Some may not know that the Lord prohibits seeking information from them, but He is very specific in this.

As for the person who turns to mediums [who consult the dead] or to spiritists, to play the prostitute after them, I shall set My face against that person and will cut him off from his people [excluding him from the atonement made for them]. ~ Leviticus 20:6 AMP.

If a person seeks the kingdom of darkness for help getting rid of spirits of darkness, the Bible guarantees it won't work. Jesus reinforces the fact that you can't use darkness to get rid of darkness.

But Jesus knew their thoughts, and said to them: "Every kingdom divided against itself is brought to desolation, and every city or house divided against itself will not stand.
~ Matthew12:25

The Bible warns us that the devil will fool many by performing signs and wonders. People can be led to believe that these signs and wonders performed by mediums (who utilize familiar spirits) are coming from God, especially when they call themselves spiritual counselors. According to the Bible, they are really employed by the devil.

These people often call themselves a 'channeler,' and that is exactly what they do; they channel evil spirits.

> When men tell you to consult mediums and spiritists, who whisper and mutter, should not a people inquire of their God? Why consult the dead on behalf of the living? If they do not speak according to this word, they have no light of dawn. ~ Isaiah 8:19-20

A familiar spirit communicates through them to tell the person what they want to hear. Familiar spirits are just that. They are familiar with the person who died or with the history of a place, and can give answers to questions that will amaze the person seeking advice.

Familiar spirits have been around since creation, so they have had a lot of practice knowing how to convince people they are a dead relative or friend. They also can produce lying signs by writing a note in the dead person's handwriting.

> The coming of the [Antichrist, the lawless] one is through the activity of Satan, [attended] with great power [all kinds of counterfeit miracles] and [deceptive] signs and false wonders [all of them lies], and by unlimited seduction to evil and with all the deception of wickedness for

those who are perishing, because they did not welcome the love of the truth [of the gospel] so as to be saved [they were spiritually blind, and rejected the truth that would have saved them].
~ *2 Thessalonians 2:9-10 (AMP)*

There are also repercussions for seeking information by reading a horoscope.

You are wearied in the multitude of your counsels; Let now the astrologers, the stargazers, and the monthly prognosticators stand up and save you from what shall come upon you. ~ *Isaiah 47:13*

This scripture implies that there will come a day we will all stand before the Lord who is the Judge of Heaven and Earth, and will have to give an account for our life. If people have been involved in these things and haven't repented, been forgiven and changed their lifestyle, it isn't going to go well for them on their day of judgment. No excuse will work. These ungodly practices and those who promote them won't be able to save a person or prevent any punishment from coming upon them for seeking their counsel. The Word of God says they stand up to give a testimony against you. God considers them 'foreign gods.'

God stands in the congregation of the mighty; he judges among the gods. ~ *Psalm 82:1*

God will be the Judge, and there will be foreign gods as witnesses in the same courtroom.

The case for the Prosecution

Then I heard a loud voice in heaven say: "Now have come the salvation and the power and the kingdom of our God, and the authority of his Messiah. For the accuser of our brothers and sisters, who accuses them before our God day and night, has been hurled down.
~ Revelation 12:10

The following fictional story takes place in a courtroom setting in heaven. It is an illustration of that day of reckoning for a believer who has been called to answer to God for possessing items in their home that the Lord prohibits. It includes a dialog between satan, as the prosecuting attorney who is presenting the charges against the Christian, and God who is the Judge.

The Prosecutor states his case: "Your honor I am here today to present evidence in the case of the kingdom of darkness vs. John Smith (made-up name) of the kingdom of light. I want to present testimony from witnesses that Smith, as a confessing believer, has chosen to keep forbidden items in his home or somewhere on his property."

The Judge will ask, "What are these items?" The Prosecutor lists the items as evidence. The items could include a Ouija board, tarot cards, a book on horoscopes (which is astrology), pornography, movies or DVD's that invite in the darkness, CD's with demonic music, and whatever other items he can find.

The Judge asks for the accuser to present witnesses who can testify in this case.

The Prosecutor calls on an angel of the Lord who has been assigned to the person. The Lord has given each of us angels to minister to us and help us. (Hebrews 1:14) It would be difficult for the angels to be required to give a testimony against the very one they are charged by the Lord to protect. The Lord has given each of us a free will, and we can use it to break His laws. If we do, we will have to pay the price for our sin.

The good news is that the angels will continue to minister to us during the times that we suffer under the consequences that follow a guilty verdict.

No matter how secret the sin is, God knows—and so does satan. The Prosecutor says, "I know that Smith doesn't think it is wrong to have these items in his possession, but both of us know that is no excuse. He has more than one Bible in his house and he goes to church. If he cared enough to know what is in that Bible concerning what You have to say about these items, he would know that You clearly point this out. As evidence to insure a guilty verdict against Smith, I present Your Word."

Nor shall you bring an abomination into your house, lest you be doomed to destruction like it. You shall utterly detest it and utterly abhor it, for it is an accursed thing. ~ *Deuteronomy 7:26*

Then the Prosecutor continues: "So on the authority of the scriptures that are written in the Bible, You have to impose a judgment against him."

Even though this is a fictional example, it is a clear picture of how things happen in the spiritual realm. The prosecutor has enough evidence for a conviction and a judgment against Smith.

Unknown to Smith, he has just become a lawful captive of the enemy because of a judgment against him in the spiritual realm. This is an example of a curse having a legal right to come upon Smith. He may not understand what is happening to him, why he is not getting answers to his prayers, why it seems as if the heavens are brass above him, and why his life is difficult instead of being blessed.

> *And your heavens which are over your head shall be bronze, and the earth which is under you shall be iron.* ~ *Deuteronomy 28:23*

The following scripture says that when the enemy brings a charge against you, acknowledge what he is saying to you, just in case he has something on you. Quickly repent before he can get your case into the Courtroom of Heaven and bring charges against you.

> *Agree with your adversary quickly, while you are on the way with him, lest your adversary deliver you to the judge, the judge hand you over to the officer, and you be thrown into prison.* ~ *Matthew 5:25*

Why should you agree with the enemy? He may be bringing a truth to you that you didn't know was a sin; and you are being given a chance to repent first. Repent quickly and ask forgiveness for any sin in your life. Next, ask the Holy Spirit to help you overcome your weakness in areas of temptation that can lead you into sin.

Once you have repented and received the Lord's forgiveness, the enemy is forced to drop his case against you, and you save yourself from repercussions that would surely affect you in the physical realm.

Until Smith realizes his sin and repents, he is susceptible to a judgment against him, even if he doesn't know his particular sin is specified in the Bible. The responsibility to read God's Word and know what it says rests upon us. As Christians and citizens of the Kingdom of Heaven, we are held accountable for our actions.

We understand that, as heaven's citizens living on this earth, we are responsible to follow the laws of the land. Break the law of the land and there are repercussions. It's the same thing in kingdom living—break spiritual laws and face consequences.

And we know that all things

work together for good to

those who love God, to those

who are the called according

to His purpose.

~ Romans 8:28

Chapter 4

Demons Bring Curses

Certain items bring demons and a curse from God upon a person or household.

> *As the bird by wandering, as the swallow by flying, so the curse causeless shall not come.*
> *~ Proverbs 26:2 KJV*

The word "come" in this scripture is significant. Its definition is found in Strong's Concordance. Among the definitions are: *to come upon, fall or light upon, attack (enemy), befall, besiege, abide.*

It is clear how this affects us. If a curse can find a legal right to come on anything or anyone, it will *come, light on, abide,* and the demons attached make themselves at home there.

Certain items will always be cursed by God. We should understand how a curse can work against us. Scripture reveals a clear and understandable process of how a curse works.

> *"You shall have no other gods before Me. You shall not make for yourself a carved image— any likeness of anything that is in heaven above, or that is in the earth beneath, or that is in*

the water under the earth; you shall not bow down to them nor serve them. For I, the Lord your God, am a jealous God, visiting the iniquity of the fathers upon the children to the third and fourth generations of those who hate Me.
~ Exodus 20:3-5.

The Bible gives us many examples of followers of "the one true God," who needlessly invited curses into their lives because of forbidden items in their possession.

One example is in Joshua, where we see the Lord warning Joshua to tell the people not to take any of the spoils of war for themselves out of the city of Jericho or they would curse themselves.

And you, by all means abstain from the accursed things, lest you become accursed when you take of the accursed things, and make the camp of Israel a curse, and trouble it.
~ Joshua 6:18

As we read further, we see what happened to those that didn't heed the warning of the Lord.

But the children of Israel committed a trespass regarding the accursed things, for Achan the son of Carmi, the son of Zabdi, the son of Zerah, of the tribe of Judah, took of the accursed things; so the anger of the Lord burned against the children of Israel. ~ Joshua 7:1

This was an act of rebellion against God. The result of taking an accursed item and bringing it into the camp caused God to withdraw His protective presence and His blessing over the Hebrew children. In their next battle they expected to win easily against the small city of Ai, but they were soundly defeated.

The Israelites quickly realized that they had angered God and knew that they would not be able to stand before any of their enemies if God wasn't on their side. They also realized that their enemies would know that the God of the Hebrew children wasn't protecting them any longer, so they would be an easy prey. The Word says the hearts of the people melted and became as water from fear.

> *And the men of Ai struck down about thirty-six men, for they chased them from before the gate as far as Shebarim, and struck them down on the descent; therefore the hearts of the people melted and became like water.* ~ *Joshua 7:5*

> *Then Joshua tore his clothes, and fell to the earth on his face before the ark of the Lord until evening, he and the elders of Israel; and they put dust on their heads. (vs. 6)*

Joshua and the elders bowed before the Lord in humility and repentance. Then Joshua inquired of the Lord to find out why they had lost the battle of Ai. In vs.11-12 the Lord speaks to Joshua and says,

> *Israel has sinned, and they have also transgressed My covenant which I commanded them. For they have even taken some of the accursed things, and have both stolen and*

deceived; and they have also put it among their own stuff. Therefore the children of Israel could not stand before their enemies, but turned their backs before their enemies, because they have become doomed to destruction. Neither will I be with you anymore, unless you destroy the accursed from among you.

This could relate to a person who feels they are under attack from the enemy, but does not have a clear understanding of the cause.

It is possible that we lose our personal battles because of cursed items we have in our homes. You may not have brought the item in yourself, and you may not be aware that it is there (like Joshua,) but it will affect everyone in the home, just as it affected the whole camp of Israel.

Because this is a spiritual battle, a person may blame satan for their problems, not realizing that there is something in their home that is causing a major conflict in the spiritual realm. When we realize we are under attack, the solution is to humble ourselves before God and seek Him, just as Joshua and the elders did.

In verse 13, the Lord answers Joshua and gives the solution:

"Get up, sanctify the people, and say, 'Sanctify yourselves for tomorrow, because thus says the Lord God of Israel: "There is an accursed thing in your midst, O Israel; you cannot stand

before your enemies until you take away the accursed thing from among you."

To sanctify means *to make holy, to consecrate, to set apart for God's service.* They broke their covenant with God. In order to come back under His spiritual and physical covenant, they had to repent and ask forgiveness.

Then it shall be that he who is taken with the accursed thing shall be burned with fire, he and all that he has, because he has transgressed the covenant of the Lord, and because he has done a disgraceful thing in Israel. (vs. 15)

Joshua gets a confession from Achan that he had stolen a garment and some silver and gold from the cursed city and buried them under his tent.

The scripture says that Achan and his whole family were punished with death because of the transgression. Because we are living under the New Covenant with Jesus as our mediator and extender of grace and mercy, we aren't physically killed because of a curse, but God still hates items that are used to exalt satan. The demons attached to them still intend harm to us.

Joshua 8:1 tells what happened after the leaders and people repented. The Lord blessed Israel and they were able to defeat Ai the next time they went out against them.

If certain items reside in our home with or without our knowledge, it gives permission to the demons to be there. We will be as guilty of breaking our covenant with the Lord as the children of Israel were. It's clear that under certain circumstances we can put God in a position where he has to allow the enemy to have access into our lives. No amount of blaming, binding or rebuking the enemy will make a difference when we are the one at fault.

When we realize there are more problems than normal coming against us, we need to seek the Lord to find out if there is an item in our homes that may have a curse attached and quickly get rid of it, just as the Israelites did.

Hedge of protection that surrounds believers

You may know that, as Christians, God has put a hedge of protection around us and our homes. There is even a scripture in Job that talks about this hedge.

> *There was a man in the land of Uz, whose name was Job; and that man was blameless and upright, and one who feared God and shunned evil.* ~ Job.1:1

In the following scripture, there is a dialog between satan and God, where satan is noting that God has placed a hedge around Job, his family and his home.

> *Have You not made a hedge around him, around his household, and around all that he has on every side? You have blessed the work of his hands, and his possessions have increased in the land.* ~ Job 1:10

It is interesting that satan had full knowledge of the hedge that God had placed around Job, and he was complaining that he basically couldn't find a gate through the hedge where he could have access to him. We can be sure that the hedge was there because of Job's righteousness.

This confirms that, as believers, if we are in right standing with God, we do have a hedge around us and our homes. Because the Lord did this for Job, he will do it for us.

But we can remove our right standing before the Lord ourselves. It is safe to say that both God and our enemy know that if a believer embraces the demonic realm in any way, it gives the thief access to us.

When things began to go wrong for Job, we see that he immediately humbled himself before the Lord and sought His face. We need to follow Job's example to find out if this is an attack because of what is in our possession, or if this is a trial of our faith. This will give us a powerful testimony to the glory of God after we come through on the other side, just as Job did.

But He knows the way that I take;
When He has tested me, I shall come forth as
gold. ~ Job 23:10

No matter which it is, a trial or an attack, if we keep our focus on the Lord He will give us the revelation we need for every situation.

And we know that all things work together for
good to those who love God, to those who are
called according to His purpose.
~ Romans 8:28

So the Lord said to him,
"What is that in your hand?"
He said, "A rod." And He said,
"Cast it on the ground." So he
cast it on the ground, and it
became a serpent; and
Moses fled from it.
~ Exodus 4:2-3

Chapter 5

Objects With A Demon Attached

There are several scriptures that tell us that idols get their life from the demons attached to them. The items have no life in themselves, so there has to be a demonic force connected in some way.

They provoked Him to jealousy with foreign gods; With abominations they provoked Him to anger. They sacrificed to demons, not to God. ~ *Deuteronomy 32:16-17*

They thought they were sacrificing to the wood or stone idol, but in reality, they were sacrificing to the demonic force that had attached itself to the idol and was empowered through its boss, the devil.

In 1 Corinthians, Paul explains that idols are really demons.

"What do I imply then? That food offered to idols is (intrinsically changed by the fact and amounts to) anything or that an idol itself is a (living) thing? I am suggesting that what the pagans sacrifice they offer (in effect) to demons—to evil spiritual powers—and not to

God (at all). I do not want you to fellowship and be partners with diabolical spirits.
~ 1 Corinthians 10:19-20 AMP

Pagan worship is a violation of a believer's union with Christ. The idols themselves hold no threat; the danger lies in the demons who, unknown to the worshippers, are the real objects of idol worship. (The Nelson Study Bible commentary)

A curse attached to a gift

One day, my husband and I got a call from a woman I will call Jane. Jane is a Christian, and she asked if we would come and pray with her and tell her what to do about an item that she had received as a gift. She had discovered that a curse was attached to it. She lived in our area, so we went over to her house to hear her story and pray with her.

The story she told us was chilling. She said that her ex-husband (who lived in a western state) had sent four decorated wooden rods to her and their three children as Christmas gifts. She said that he was a Native American and he thought it would be a nice gift to remind the children of their heritage. He sent one along for her too.

When she received them, she stood them in the corner of the dining room. They were very pretty with all of the beading, feathers and other decorations. She didn't give them much thought. That is until she invited several friends over for Christmas dinner. One of the guests saw the rods and asked Jane if she knew what the different symbolic items on each rod meant.

Jane realized that she didn't have a clue. The woman told her she had a friend who was a Native American Chief and she would like to take the rods to him and see if he could tell her what the symbolism on each one meant. Jane thought that would be a great idea, so the woman took the rods home with her that day and went to visit the Chief.

He told her that the items on the children's rods all carried with them traditional Native American blessings, but Jane's rod had a curse of death attached to it. Hers had a pretty white feather on it with unusual red dots on the feather. He told her that the white feather with the red spots on it meant death to the owner. The spots were spots of blood. He recommended that it be burned or destroyed. She told him that it didn't belong to her and that she would take it back to the owner to get rid of it. He warned her to be careful, because it could affect her as it was in her possession.

On her way back to Jane's house she had to stop to get gas. Her credit card wouldn't work in the gas pump. The screen on the pump said to see the attendant. As she was walking across the lot from the pumps to go into the store, a car backing out didn't see her and hit her. It knocked her down and almost ran her over. She ended up with a broken hip and had to have surgery.

While she was in the Emergency Room waiting for x-ray results, she gave Jane a call and asked her if she would go and get her car. She related the story the Chief had told her and suggested that Jane take the rods and destroy them immediately.

That's when we got the call. So there we were a couple of hours later, looking at the rods and a fearful woman. She prayed with us regarding the curse that came with the rods. She repented to the Lord for receiving a curse into her home that came with the rods. She asked forgiveness from the Lord and asked that He remove the curse from her and her home.

We commanded any demons who had come with the curse to leave. We thanked the Lord that there would be no repercussions upon any of us as we destroyed the rods. Then we took all of the rods out and burned them. We have learned that when someone puts a curse on something, sometimes they curse the person who breaks the curse, so we also prayed Psalm 91 over ourselves.

I am not saying the rods that the kids received with the blessing on them were cursed; it would depend on the source of the blessings. Different people pray to different gods and we aren't in any position to judge the person who made them. At that point, Jane didn't want anything to do with them. She was not about to take any chances. Her children were upset at first, but then when she explained it to them they were okay.

When she called the father of the children and told him what she had found out and of the consequences, he denied all knowledge of any curses. He said that he had asked a friend to make the rods and had just briefly looked at them before mailing them. Whether he was telling the truth or not, doesn't change the fact that a curse was attached and demons were behind it to bring about death.

Not all rods are demonic

Rods, in themselves, are scriptural. In the Bible they are called mat-teh's. God himself called the rod that Moses had the "Rod of God".

Even though the mat-teh' was an inanimate object, God used them for His purposes. This example gives us scriptural proof that, even though the rod itself is lifeless, it can have a spiritual supernatural life force attached to it.

> So the Lord said to him, "What is that in your hand?" He said, "A rod." And He said, "Cast it on the ground." So he cast it on the ground, and it became a serpent; and Moses fled from it. ~ Exodus 4:2-3

There were magicians in the story who also had rods in their hands to use for their purposes, and they clearly weren't from the same God as Moses. It is not unusual for the enemy to use scriptural items in ceremonies because of the symbolism and its importance for good or bad. He uses them to promote demonic occult practices. The devil is the great counterfeiter. He can't create anything so he has to copy and use things for his own purposes.

I am the good shepherd; and I know My sheep, and am known by My own. As the Father knows Me, even so I know the Father; and I lay down My life for the sheep. And other sheep I have which are not of this fold; them also I must bring, and they will hear My voice; and there will be one flock and one shepherd.

~John 10:14-16 NIV

Chapter 6

You Can Purchase a Curse

What if a person buys something that has a curse attached and they don't know it., can it affect them? The answer is yes. We see from the previous testimony a curse can come with a gift. They can also come with an item you purchase. When you bring that item home, you bring the curse and demons with it. Demons don't care if you are a Christian or not.

I have a personal testimony about innocently buying an item that had a curse attached.

Many years ago, my husband and I decided to purchase a travel trailer to fix up and re-sell to make a profit to pay our property taxes that year. I found a beautiful travel trailer for sale, parked in the driveway of a nice home in an upscale neighborhood of our town. The woman told me she was selling it for her parents. They were out of state, and she needed to sell it quickly because she wasn't allowed to have it in her driveway for more than two weeks. I was able to buy it at a great price for its age and condition. It only needed some cabinet repair and new carpet.

We purchased the trailer, pulled it home and put it in our backyard where we would work on it the next day.

That night as I was falling asleep, I thought I heard screaming and yelling in my mind. I tried rebuking it, but couldn't get it to leave. I prayed for the Lord to remove it, but the noise in my head continued. I told my husband about it and he wondered if the trailer we bought had a curse attached. We asked the Lord why I was hearing the voices. The Holy Spirit told me that we bought and paid for three curses that came with the trailer, a curse of alcoholism, a curse of contention, and a curse of divorce. They had a legal right to come on us because we bought and paid for them along with the trailer.

We immediately repented for not seeking the Lord first, and then repented for the sin of purchasing these three curses. We asked the Lord's forgiveness, and we asked the Lord to wash us and the travel trailer with the blood of Jesus and set us, and it, free of any curses or demons. We then commanded any curse to be broken and any demons that came with it to leave.

After praying, I was able to fall asleep with no problem. The yelling voices were gone. You may wonder why I heard the voices. I believe the Lord opened my spiritual ears to hear what was going on in the spiritual realm.

We should have prayed about the trailer before buying it. If we had, we could have taken care of any curses at that time. We came to realize later that it had happened this way for a purpose. The testimony turned out to be useful for future ministry.

The next morning I went to the woman's house where I had purchased the trailer. I asked her if she could tell me the history of the trailer. She said that it was a sad story. Her parents were both alcoholics. They had lived in the trailer in a mobile home park. They had been kicked out of the park because of their drinking, fighting and yelling at each other. They were now living in separate states and in the process of getting a divorce.

God speaks to each of us

I have shared this testimony at various times and someone always asks, "Why can't I hear like that"? The answer to that question would be that God is always speaking, but most people are not listening. Some explain His voice away, thinking it is their own mind.

To hear His voice, you need to get closer to the Lord, study His Word, and pray to Him on a consistent basis. Ask Him for a more personal relationship. Ask the Lord to help you to be more sensitive to the different ways that He speaks to you. Ask the Holy Spirit for His gifts, and as you mature, you can begin to operate in them.

He speaks to different people in different, often unusual ways. Don't limit the Holy Spirit in how He wants to communicate with you.

Just as Moses saw the burning bush and heard the voice of the Lord speaking to Him out of it, we can hear spiritually if the Lord opens our ears to it. We will be able to see into the spiritual realm if He opens the eyes of our understanding, as He did for Moses.

And the Angel of the Lord appeared to him in a flame of fire from the midst of a bush. So he looked, and behold, the bush was burning with fire, but the bush was not consumed...: So when the Lord saw that he turned aside to look, God called to him from the midst of the bush and said, "Moses, Moses!" And he said, "Here I am." ~ Exodus 3:2,4

For He is our God, And we are the people of His pasture, and the sheep of His hand. Today, if you will hear His voice: "Do not harden your hearts, as in the rebellion, As in the day of trial in the wilderness, ~ Psalms 95:7-8

He is not saying that He might speak to us, but that He will speak to us.

I am the good shepherd; and I know My sheep, and am known by My own. As the Father knows Me, even so I know the Father; and I lay down My life for the sheep. And other sheep I have which are not of this fold; them also I must bring, and they will hear My voice; and there will be one flock and one shepherd.
~ John 10:14-16 NIV

We only need to be willing to listen for his voice. Just make sure you don't second-guess what you hear until you can't hear anymore. The Lord is no respecter of persons. What He has done for one He will do for another. We just have to ask and expect to receive.

And Elisha prayed, and said, "Lord, I pray, open his eyes that he may see." Then the Lord opened the eyes of the young man,

and he saw. And behold, the mountain was full of horses and chariots of fire all around Elisha.
~ 2 Kings 6:17;

This was the angelic host of heaven ready to defend and fight for Elisha and his servant. They were unseen to the natural eye, but visible in the spiritual realm.

The following is a prayer you can pray often, if you want to hear the voice of the Lord and see in the spirit with the eyes of your understanding.

Dear Heavenly Father,

I come before you humbly, repenting for the times in my life when You were speaking to me but I wasn't listening. I ask forgiveness for that. Please help me to hear Your voice. I ask that You would extend Your grace and mercy to me, and open the eyes of my understanding so I can see clearly what you want to show me. Please open my spiritual ears to hear.

I ask you to give me Your spirit of wisdom that I will need to process the revelations that You are going to show me and tell me.

Please guide me clearly in what I am to do with what I will see and hear. I thank You that in Your Word You say that in these last days, dreams and visions will increase. I ask that You would give me knowledge to be able to interpret them for Your purposes, just as You did for Joseph.

I thank You, Lord, for loving me and continuing to guide me along the path of the destiny that You have planned for me. Amen.

Curses attached to some collections

I am including this because some people innocently have collections of things that could bring unwanted results. By itself an item isn't a problem, but too much of a good thing can turn into a bad thing called idolatry. We don't want anything to appear to take the place of Jesus or come between us and Him.

We often see a collection of angels in people's homes. People don't realize that filling their homes with angel pictures and statues doesn't give the angels pleasure, and it doesn't please God.

The amount of angel statues in a home does not make a home safe, as some people tell me. In fact, some of these people weren't Christians but were comforted by having angels in their home, thinking in some way that God would bless because of the presence of these angels.

In reality, this would be a grief to real angels because it turns the house into an altar to them. In the Word we see that an angel rebukes John for thinking too highly of him.

> *And I fell at his feet to worship him. But he said to me, "See that you do not do that! I am your fellow servant, and of your brethren who have the testimony of Jesus. Worship God! For the testimony of Jesus is the spirit of prophecy."*
> *~ Revelation 19:10*

My intent is to educate, not to offend or to judge anyone who may have a home full of statues of angels, or any collection. I realize that if a person buys one angel and puts it in their house and others see it, it gives them something to buy as a gift for that person. A person can find themselves loaded with gifts of angels and they don't want to hurt anyone's feelings by getting rid of them.

There are some collections that don't have a spiritual connotation. One example would be a collection of bells. A collection of bells in your house doesn't mean you worship bells. Just be alert to the individual item, and what it may mean in the spiritual realm. Something like owls, however, may be a problem. Owls are known to be creatures of the night. If a person has a house full of owls, it won't make them wise, but may attract darkness.

Souvenirs from other countries

Carved statues or other artifacts that come home from foreign lands may be a problem. Sometimes they are gifts from someone who went on a mission trip or vacation. These gifts might seem to be innocent objects, but they may not be as innocent as you may think. They may have curses or demons attached.

I have been in homes of Christians who have statues from foreign countries sitting around. When asked about it, they say a missionary has given it to them, or their parents brought it to them as a gift from a foreign country. They don't realize that witches and witch doctors in those countries choose to curse such objects to specifically get at Christians..

Nor shall you bring an abomination into your house, lest you be doomed to destruction like it. You shall utterly detest it and utterly abhor it, for it is an accursed thing. ~ Deuteronomy 7:26

I am not saying that every statue from a foreign country is cursed. I am saying you need to pray over it. On one of our trips to West Africa, I was searching for souvenirs to bring home. I picked up a carved elephant. The pastor who lived there was with us and said, "We have to pray over that." He went on to tell us that witch doctors curse them to bring trouble to people buying them, especially Christians. We prayed over it then I bought it.

One time we were sharing testimonies at church about different things that had happened as we were going through houses to spiritually cleanse them. A couple shared that they had a bronze Buddha that had been given to them years earlier, before they became Christians. They didn't think anything about it until they began to hear about spiritually cleansing their home. They knew right away they needed to get rid of it, but didn't want to throw it away where someone might get hold of it. They decided to throw it into a lake by their house. They shared that when they threw it, as it was sailing through the air, it laughed all the way, until it went into the water! They were one convinced couple.

Another time, I was in the office of a pastor and noticed that he had a shelf that ran around the room about 12 inches down from the ceiling. On the shelf were ugly carved little statues, sitting in the highest place in the room. I noticed that the rest of the room was decorated nicely with spiritual pictures and other items that pointed to Christ.

I asked him about the statues and he said that different missionaries had given them to him as gifts over the years. I asked him if he had prayed and broken any curses off the statues. He just laughed and said no, that he didn't believe in that stuff. I am sad to say that pastor was removed from his position in that church within two years, and several years after that went through a divorce. I often wondered how much effect his attitude about the spiritual realm had to do with the enemy having a legal right in his life to destroy him.

I think if the people realized there were demons attached to the keepsakes in their homes or offices, it wouldn't be so hard to part with them. It may sound harsh, but when you have had experience with this type of thing, as I have, it is hard to sugar coat it in any way. It is just plain dangerous.

Then He arose and rebuked the wind, and said to the sea, "Peace, be still!" And the wind ceased and there was a great calm.

~ Mark 4:36-39

Chapter 7

Demons Influence and Manipulate

The following scripture reveals how demonic forces can affect our atmosphere.

Now when they had left the multitude, they took Him along in the boat as He was. And other little boats were also with Him. And a great windstorm arose, and the waves beat into the boat, so that it was already filling. But He was in the stern, asleep on a pillow. And they awoke Him and said to Him, "Teacher, do You not care that we are perishing?" Then He arose and rebuked the wind, and said to the sea, "Peace, be still!" And the wind ceased and there was a great calm. ~ Mark 4:36-39

Jesus addressed the spirits behind the storm, the wind and the sea, and they had to obey.

Testimony

A group from our church was asked to pray through the house of a Christian couple. They had a teenage daughter who was having problems sleeping at night. The daughter had been awakened several nights by a spiritual being standing beside her bed. She was terrified and told her parents that this was something real. She was afraid to go to sleep without a light on.

They said there had been other manifestations in the home that caused the dogs to bark at seemingly nothing. The hair on the dogs backs would go up and, at times, their eyes would track something only they could see.

They had instances of objects being moved around. They would even put certain things in specific places on purpose, and then find, when no one was home or during the night, those items had been moved.

When we went through the house we did find some scary movies in the daughter's bedroom, but the biggest surprise was in the bedroom of the grandmother who was living with them. We removed bags of movies that were full of demonic subjects. She loved to watch scary movies and she didn't think there was anything wrong with it. She didn't believe that demons could come attached to anything. She considered herself a Christian, but those movies that promoted the darkness interested her for some reason.

When they thought about it, the problem of hearing movement in the house, having items moved around, and the dogs barking for seemingly no reason, had started when the grandmother had moved in. Once everything suspect was removed, the daughter could sleep again and the animals relaxed and stopped their barking.

It caused the daughter to rededicate her life to the Lord. Unfortunately, the grandma got angry and moved out. But their home was peaceful once again. They are praying in faith for the grandmother to get an understanding of how these things are affecting her whole life.

Curses attached to people

One prayer assignment that stands out to me happened several years later. This is a testimony of how demons can be attached to people who come into your house to visit, and how they can be a hidden source for problems that affect those living in the house.

A couple shared with us that they were having problems in their home with something that was scaring their kids at night. They had built the home, so they were the first ones to live in the house.

Shortly after moving in, their children had problems sleeping. The children would wake up in the night and see dark figures in their room. They would freak out, screaming, and run to the parent's room and everyone would be awake all night. It didn't happen to just one of the kids; it would be first one and then the other.

We had a special prayer session about the problem. We started by asking the couple if they remembered when this problem began. We asked if someone had come into the home that wasn't a believer in Jesus, but they couldn't think of anyone at that time. We walked through the house to see if we could find anything that would open a spiritual door that would welcome these intruders. We walked through each room with them but couldn't find anything that would attract the kingdom of darkness.

We began to pray and ask the Lord about the source of the problem. As we prayed, I saw a picture in my mind of their property. It was fenced all around, with a gate at the entrance of the driveway. Their property was indeed fenced and gated. In the vision, I saw wolves walking the perimeter of the fence. They were looking for a way in.

In the vision, I saw a woman driving a convertible with the top down pull up to the gate. Then the wolves jump up into the car. The wolves didn't attack the woman; they were all greeting her as if they were domesticated dogs that belonged to her. I could see their tails wagging and they were taking turns giving her a lick on the cheek. Next, I saw the gate open for her to drive in. The wolves switched their attention to the house as she drove the car down the driveway. The wolves were hanging out of the car, looking at the house with grins of anticipation on their faces. It was as if they were thinking of the little lambs in that house.

As the woman got out of the car and walked up to the front door, the wolves jumped out and walked right up to the door with her. She opened the door as if she lived there and walked in. The wolves walked right in with her.

I related what I was seeing and asked if they knew who the woman could be, as she appeared to have access to their home. Instantly they knew who it was.

The Holy Spirit brought to their minds that the first time the problem had occurred with the kids was when his mother had come to visit for a few days. The kids hadn't slept well and kept waking up crying. They remembered that even though no one else in the house had slept the night through, the mom had commented at breakfast that she had slept fine.

From that time on, the kids would still occasionally wake up scared and tell their parents they were seeing dark figures in their rooms, or if they got up in the night, they would see the figures in the hallway. The kids were afraid to get up in the night, even go to the bathroom, for fear of seeing these dark creatures in the hallway.

As they thought about this, they remembered it seemed that whenever his mother would come to visit, the problem always got worse. The kids would all end up sleeping in their parent's room, which meant they didn't get any sleep either. The mother never complained of losing any sleep.

It also seemed to them that whenever the grandmother was staying with them, within a short time, they would all end up snapping at each other. It turned out she was involved in a different religion and didn't believe that Jesus was the only way into heaven. She didn't agree with her son and his wife's views on God and Jesus at all. Even though she didn't openly dispute their faith with them any longer, they stayed away from the subject because in the past, they had arguments with her about their way of life. Any discussion just opened up trouble. They wanted to respect her as a parent, but wouldn't compromise their spiritual beliefs to please her.

As the revelation came, they shared that she had called that day to tell them that she would be there for a few days the next week. We asked the Holy Spirit how we should pray about this problem. We all prayed in tongues because, when you don't know how to pray the Holy Spirit within you knows how and what to pray. (Romans 8:26-27)

This helps us to get the mind of God about the issue and keep our personal opinions out of the prayer.

We began to get a direction. The son began to decree that any spirit that came onto the property with his mother had to stay with her. They were to be bound to her and not free to move about the house while she was there. When she left, they had to go with her. He prayed and added that if there was anything demonic left over from her past visits in their home, it had to leave now. Then we went through each room, anointing it with oil and commanding anything that was not of God to leave. We asked the Holy Spirit to fill the house and bring peace.

You may wonder why we didn't tell the evil spirits they couldn't come into the house with his mother. We realized that these spirits were welcomed by her, so we didn't have spiritual jurisdiction to control what she allowed. However, we could control their actions when they came onto the property and into the home.

The next week arrived and she came for her visit. The couple was anxious to see what would happen. That first night everyone slept great. The mom got up the next morning and said that she hadn't slept a wink. She thought maybe it was the travel and she had been overtired.

Everyone slept great the next night. When she came to breakfast she complained that she hadn't slept a wink. She announced that she would stay at a hotel from now on when she came to visit. She told them that she was used to getting up in the night reading, eating and moving about and didn't want to wake anyone up.

The result of our prayer was that the spirits that had been keeping the kids awake were now keeping her awake. We have prayed for her over the years for a revelation from God to reveal Himself to her, but that is in the Lord's hands.

There is an example from the Bible that shows how demons in one person not only affects them, but others around them.

And when they had come to the multitude, a man came to Him, kneeling down to Him and saying, "Lord, have mercy on my son, for he is an epileptic and suffers severely; for he often falls into the fire and often into the water. So I brought him to Your disciples, but they could not cure him." Then Jesus answered and said, "O faithless and perverse generation, how long shall I be with you? How long shall I bear with you? Bring him here to Me." And Jesus rebuked the demon, and it came out of him; and the child was cured from that very hour.
~ Matthew 17:14-18

I am sure that the parents of this boy were constantly on edge wondering what their son would do next. They were emotionally and physically affected because of the demons that were attacking their son. Others would be affected too because the scripture says he would throw himself into the fire or the water often. I wouldn't want to babysit him! Whether the parents knew it was due to a demonic influence is not clear, but the disciples and Jesus knew the hidden source of the boy's problems.

Testimony regarding a family keepsake

I received this testimony after a retreat where I had talked of covenanting your home to the Lord, and the need to cleanse it from possible curses.

Dear Jeanette, I felt a huge tug as you spoke at the Retreat concerning people having things that carry curses. God brought to my remembrance a porcelain doll my mother asked me to hold for her. She had made the doll in a class many years ago. The doll had been in the homes of different relatives, and was now in my attic.

After God showed me that the doll carried a curse, I marched straight up to the attic. The moment I started walking toward the doll I felt as if I was suffocating. My heart started to race. As I bent over to grab the doll, the eyes appeared to be staring at me. I grabbed that doll by the arm and took it outside to the trash can. God told me to smash her on the cement. It didn't break easily— just the arm came off. I put it in the trash can.

A while later, the Lord told me to get the doll and take it to the garbage cans out back. It was then that I saw a bag stuffed inside her left arm. This was alarming. Who would stuff a bag into a doll's arm? I knew immediately that it had to do with voodoo. I took the doll out back and smashed it to the ground with all my might. It wouldn't break! Finally, each limb broke at the joints (knees & wrists).There was a bag in each limb. One bag broke open a little bit and horrible odor came out. I saw part of the bag and it had a skull on it, like a voodoo doll. The Lord showed me that doll carried curses of sickness and death. I smashed it completely and put it in trash.

Later I asked my Mom if she had put bags in the dolls arms when she made it, but she said she hadn't and didn't know anything about them. When I asked the Holy Spirit who had implanted the cursed bags, He gave me a vision of who had done this, and now that person is on my prayer list.

After removing that doll from my property, my husband and I took Holy Communion and covenanted our house to the Lord. When we went back into our home, I felt a huge cloud lift off my house and I felt such a peace. My two-year-old daughter grabbed a tabret and started singing and praising! What a shift in the atmosphere! Praise God for His mercy.

*The angel of
the Lord encamps
all around those
who fear Him, And
delivers them.*
~ Psalm 34:7

Chapter 8

Angels In Our Homes

The Word says that angels are commissioned by Him to minister to the heirs of salvation, so it is reasonable to conclude they would inhabit a believer's home.

Are they not all ministering spirits sent forth to minister for those who will inherit salvation?
~ Hebrews 1:14

Just as there can be demonic forces at work in our homes, there are good spiritual beings around us called angels, also affecting our atmosphere.

Angels are spiritual entities that can physically appear and speak with people, eat food, and help fight battles. We are encouraged by these confirming scriptures that there is a heavenly host assigned to us as believers. They assist us and minister to us, even though we don't see them with our earthly eyes.

We see the Angel of the Lord encouraging Gideon:

And the Angel of the Lord appeared to him, and said to him, "The Lord is with you, you mighty man of valor!" ~ Judges 6:12

The angel of the Lord encamps all around those who fear Him, And delivers them.
~ Psalm 34:7

Bless the Lord, you His angels, Who excel in strength, who do His word, Heeding the voice of His word. Bless the Lord, all you His hosts, You ministers of His, who do His pleasure.
~ Psalm 103:20-21

The Lord has opened the eyes of many to be able to see angels. This is not to say that a person should spend time asking God to let them see angels.

I heard the testimony of a retired pastor who shared his story of seeing an angelic presence in his home. He said that one day as he was praising the Lord, he suddenly saw an angel with his natural eyes, standing in his living room with one of his wings hanging down in such a way that it appeared the angel was injured. He asked the Lord why the angel was there, and why it appeared that he was injured. The Holy Spirit told him that the angel had heard the praise and worship music and had come to be strengthened by it.

The Holy Spirit asked the pastor if he would be willing to turn his house into an angel field hospital for the angels who were fighting over the city. The Holy Spirit explained that the angels could come to his house and be strengthened by the praise and worship, then go back out to the battle with renewed vigor.

The pastor said he would be honored to do that, but what did he need to do? The Holy Spirit told him to play the Christian radio station 24 hours a day. The angels would come to the praise music and the sound of the Word being spoken and be strengthened to go back out to the battle. So, the pastor has continued to do that. He has the radio on a Christian station and lets it play softly 24 hours a day.

Even though there isn't validation in the Word about wounded angels, we do know from reading Daniel 10:9-14, that the angel was delayed 21 days when coming in response to Daniel's prayers.

"And you shall take the anointing oil, and anoint the tabernacle and all that is in it; and you shall hallow it and all its utensils, and it shall be holy.

~ Exodus 40:9

Chapter 9

Anointing Your Home

Why should we anoint our homes? There are several instances in scripture that address dedicating a home. One is in Deuteronomy, and talks of not going to war without first dedicating a new home.

"Then the officers shall speak to the people, saying: 'What man is there who has built a new house and has not dedicated it? Let him go and return to his house, lest he die in the battle and another man dedicate it. ~ Deuteronomy 20:5

Another is found in Psalm 30:1-12. The Psalm was written to be sung at the dedication of the Temple. The following is a commentary from Adam Clarke's Commentary from the New Testament of our Lord and Saviour Jesus Christ:

A Psalm or Song at the Dedication of the House of David - it is evident that it was a custom in Israel to dedicate a new house to God with prayer, praise, and thanksgiving; and this was done in order to secure the Divine presence and blessing, for no pious or sensible man could imagine he could dwell safely in a house that was not under the immediate protection of God. ... At the times of dedication among the Jews, besides prayer and praise, a feast was made to which the relatives and neighbors were invited. Something of this custom is observed in some parts of our own country in what is called housewarming; but in these cases, the feasting only is kept up - the prayer and praise forgotten! so that the dedication appears to be rather more to Bacchus than to Jehovah, the author of every good and perfect gift.

How do you "dedicate" your home?

The Bible speaks of anointing the tabernacle that Moses built in the desert to "consecrate it." The New Testament tells us that we are the tabernacle of the Lord, but it seems appropriate that we dedicate the place where we live and "consecrate" it.

We see in Exodus that the Lord gives Moses instructions to make a holy oil for the anointing.

> *And you shall make from these a holy anointing oil, an ointment compounded according to the art of the perfumer. It shall be a holy anointing oil. With it you shall anoint the tabernacle of meeting and the ark of the Testimony.*
> ~ *Exodus 30:-25-26*

> *And you shall take the anointing oil, and anoint the tabernacle and all that is in it; and you shall hallow it and all its utensils, and it shall be holy.*
> ~ *Exodus 40:9*

It is also important to anoint the foundation stones of a home, praying as you do this, asking the Lord to remove all memory of trauma, and cleansing them of all evil witnesses. Then speak a blessing over the foundation. That foundation will stand as a witness of the Lord's blessing, for according to the scripture, the stones have memory.

And Joshua said to all the people, "Behold, this stone shall be a witness to us, for it has heard all the words of the Lord which He spoke to us. It shall therefore be a witness to you, lest you deny your God."~ Joshua 24:27

When we anoint our doorposts with the symbol of the Blood of Jesus Christ, it represents our covenant with Him. Our homes then have an outward sign for the spiritual realm to see, and establishes that the house has not only been sanctified, consecrated, and dedicated to the Lord, but covenanted to Him also.

Now the blood shall be a sign for you on the houses where you are. And when I see the blood, I will pass over you; and the plague shall not be on you to destroy you when I strike the land of Egypt.

~Exodus 12:13

Chapter 10

Preparation

There are a number of things to consider before you dedicate your home to the Lord:

- Are you having any of the problems we have noted? If so, you may want to gather a few believers you know are strong in the Lord to help you.

- If there are no problems that need to be specifically addressed, you could do the anointing yourself or with a family member or friend.

- It is important to note that you should NOT cleanse the home of a non-believer. If at least one of the people who live in the house is a believer, that person can be the gatekeeper.

Use wisdom

Here is a testimony I received from someone who had attended one of my sessions about cleansing your home:

My name is Mark. When I was at my grandma's one day, she told me that a neighbor had asked her if she had anything strange going on in her house. The neighbor said that the piano in her house would play when no one was sitting at it. One day she heard a noise in her kitchen and when she went to see where the sound was coming from, all of the countertops were dripping water, even though the sink was dry. She also said that once while standing at the sink doing dishes, something grabbed her ankles and pulled her feet out from under her and she crashed to the floor. Now her children were seeing figures of people in the house.

My grandma asked me if I would go over to her house and pray for the woman. I thought it would be exciting, so I said I would do it. I went over to the woman's house and the first thing I asked was if she or her husband were believers in Jesus Christ. She said that neither she nor her husband were religious.

I knew the scripture said that if you delivered a demon out of a person, and that person didn't take personal responsibility to fill that space with the presence of God, then the demon would try to come back into the person. If the demon saw that the person hadn't done anything to protect themselves, such as filling the space the demon had vacated by developing a closer relationship with the Lord and the Holy Spirit, then it would bring more demons back with it. I reasoned that if it could happen to a person it could apply to a house too.

> "When an unclean spirit goes out of a man, he goes through dry places, seeking rest; and finding none, he says, 'I will return to my house from which I came.' And when he comes, he finds it swept and put in order. Then he goes and takes with him seven other spirits more wicked than himself, and they enter and dwell

there; and the last state of that man is worse than the first." ~ Luke 11:24-26

I asked her if she would like to make a commitment to Jesus Christ at that time. She said that she wasn't ready to do that yet. I explained that I wouldn't be doing her any favors if I exercised authority over the demons to make them leave, because the Bible says that if you clean spirits out and don't fill that vacated space with a life that belongs to Christ, then the spirits will come back worse than before. It's sad to say that, at that time, the woman chose the demons over Jesus.

Anointing oil

To anoint the inside of your home, you can use olive oil. Oil is a symbol of the Holy Spirit. The Spirit of the Lord and the oil of anointing are linked together in the Bible. As we anoint our home with oil, we are saying that the Holy Spirit resides in this home with power, and we are dedicating this home to the ministry of the Lord. Jesus refers to the Holy Spirit as the one who has anointed Him with power.

> *"The Spirit of the Lord is upon Me, Because He has anointed Me to preach the gospel to the poor; He has sent Me to heal the brokenhearted, to proclaim liberty to the captives and recovery of sight to the blind, to set at liberty those who are oppressed;.."*
> *~ Luke 4:18*

To anoint their homes, most Christians dip their finger in olive oil and smear it on the top doorpost of each room. You can also put it on the window frames, the walls, and any objects; be led by the Holy Spirit as to what should be anointed. When doing this, you declare that the place is consecrated and dedicated to the Lord, holy and set apart for His service. You can also use the mixture I recommend for the outside of the house.

As oil symbolizes the Holy Spirit, the communion wine or juice symbolizes the blood of Jesus and our covenant God. In the Old Testament, the shedding of blood was required to seal a covenant (Hebrews 9:22). They got that blood from sacrificing an unblemished lamb. In the New Testament, the symbol of covenant with God is still the blood. Jesus is described in the Bible as the unblemished, sinless Lamb of God who provides atonement for our sins.

The next day John saw Jesus coming toward him, and said, "Behold! The Lamb of God who takes away the sin of the world!" ~ John 1:29

There is a portion of scripture that speaks to covenanting our homes to the Lord. It says to place the blood upon the doorposts of our homes as a sign to the spiritual realm that we, and our homes, are under the protection of the covenant of the Lord.

Now the blood shall be a sign for you on the houses where you are. And when I see the blood, I will pass over you; and the plague shall

not be on you to destroy you when I strike the
land of Egypt. ~ *Exodus 12:13*

Today we take communion with juice or wine as a symbol of the blood of Jesus, and the bread represents His body. We do this for our human tabernacle, so we should do this for the place where we live, as a tabernacle of God's presence.

In the following scripture, the Lord says this is important and needs to be done throughout the generations.

And you shall take a bunch of hyssop, dip it in the blood that is in the basin, and strike the lintel and the two doorposts with the blood that is in the basin. And none of you shall go out of the door of his house until morning. For the Lord will pass through to strike the Egyptians; and when He sees the blood on the lintel and on the two doorposts, the Lord will pass over the door and not allow the destroyer to come into your houses to strike you. And you shall observe this thing as an ordinance for you and your sons forever. ~ *Exodus 12:22-24*

He uses the word ordinance. That word means a 'decree that is a law.' The blood hasn't lost its power to cleanse sin, heal and set free. This applies to the hearts of people, the heart of the land, and the heart of your home.

We anoint the doorposts inside the home with olive oil. For the outside entrance doors, we use a mix of olive oil and hyssop oil, along with the communion element of wine or juice. Directions in scripture for anointing specify using hyssop. Hyssop is known as an anti-fungal and is used as a blood cleanser.

You can add a Mezuzah as a symbol of Blessing

As an addition to dedicating, sanctifying and covenanting your home to the Lord, a person can place a Mezuzah on the doorpost. A mezuzah is a rolled parchment scroll inscribed with Biblical passages and enclosed in a decorative case. It is affixed to the outside doorframe, and sometimes in every room in a Jewish home used for "honorable dwelling," (which would exclude a bathroom.) It fulfills the Biblical commandment to inscribe the words of the Shema "on the door posts of your house" (Deuteronomy 6:9). The word mezuzah in Hebrew means "doorpost."

The holders come in all different types and sizes. They can be out of wood or polished stones or shiny or dull clay. You can see many styles on our website www.gloriouscreations.net

The outer box holds a scroll with the following blessing known as the Sh'ma (pronounced Sha-Mah.). Sh'ma means God's blessings.

Hear, O Israel: The Lord our God, the Lord is one! You shall love the Lord your God with all your heart, with all your soul, and with all your strength.

And these words which I command you today shall be in your heart. You shall teach them diligently to your children, and shall talk of them when you sit in your house, when you walk by the way, when you lie down, and when you rise up. You shall bind them as a sign on your hand, and they shall be as frontlets between your eyes. You shall write them on the doorposts of your house and on your gates.
~ Deuteronomy 6:4-9

'And it shall be that if you earnestly obey My commandments which I command you today, to love the Lord your God and serve Him with all your heart and with all your soul, then I will give you the rain for your land in its season, the early rain and the latter rain, that you may gather in your grain, your new wine, and your oil. And I will send grass in your fields for your livestock, that you may eat and be filled.' "Take heed to yourselves, lest your heart be deceived, and you turn aside and serve other gods and worship them, lest the Lord's anger be aroused against you, and He shut up the heavens so that there be no rain, and the land yield no produce, and you perish quickly from the good land which the Lord is giving you.

"Therefore you shall lay up these words of mine in your heart and in your soul, and bind them as a sign on your hand, and they shall be

as frontlets between your eyes. You shall teach them to your children, speaking of them when you sit in your house, when you walk by the way, when you lie down, and when you rise up. And you shall write them on the doorposts of your house and on your gates, that your days and the days of your children may be multiplied in the land of which the Lord swore to your fathers to give them, like the days of the heavens above the earth.

~ Deuteronomy 11:13-21

If you decide you would like to have a mezuzah, directions for attaching it to your doorpost are in the Appendix.

Chapter 11

Housecleaning

Begin your spiritual house cleaning with a prayer of intercession on behalf of yourselves. Often the team will take communion before they begin, to seal the prayer and dedication.

If your cleansing prayer concerns an apartment, God will honor your prayer as you dedicate and consecrate your living area. You sow money into a rental lease agreement, so you have legal authority over what you are paying for. You can intercede for others in the building, but there doesn't seem to be anywhere in the Bible where someone has the authority to cast spirits out of other people's property. You can pray through the apartments of other believers, if you are invited to do so.

As you pray the spiritual cleansing prayer, substitute the appropriate word for your location, whether it is a home or business.

Dear Heavenly Father,

We humbly come before you to repent for any sin that any one of us may have committed against You that would give the enemy a legal right that allows him in our lives.

We ask that You would forgive us, and that You would wash us clean with the blood of Jesus. As we are forgiven, we ask You to move us from any Judgment to the Throne of Grace and Mercy, removing every veil from the eyes of our understanding, particularly as we go through and spiritually cleanse this home.

We ask that Your Holy Spirit clearly alert us to any objects that may have a curse attached that may be causing problems for those who live here.

We stand in the gap for this dwelling on behalf of any sins that have been committed in it from the first day of its construction until now. We ask forgiveness for those sins. We ask You to anoint us with a gift of discernment as we go through each room. Open our spiritual eyes and ears to the spiritual realm. Please direct us to any item that may be attached to anything demonic.

We thank You that You have appointed this day for our home to be cleansed, set free, sanctified, anointed and covenanted with You. As You are present in this place, please guide, direct, illuminate and empower us to do good works for You, and to overcome the enemy and continue to keep him out of our home. Amen

Then begin your walk through

Now you are ready to walk through the home. Be sure to include the garage, attic, and storage areas. As you work your way through, room by room, if you are lead to any particular items that doesn't feel right spiritually but you don't think they need to be thrown away, you can pray this example of a prayer (or one that you feel comfortable praying.)

Dear Heavenly Father, we lift this _____ to You. We make intercession on behalf of any sin that could be connected in any way to this item that has allowed a curse to attach itself to it.

We ask forgiveness for the sin and ask that you wash this_____ clean with the blood of Jesus. We command any demons that have joined themselves with the curse to this _____ to leave now, in the name of Jesus. You no longer have a job. You are fired, Go.

Father we pray that this _____ will now be a blessing to those who live here, in Jesus name. Amen

As you walk from room to room, you can put the items in a box that you think should be disposed of, and say one prayer to cover them all.

Some items might not fit in a box. We were in one home that had a very large ornate antique desk that had come out of a Governor's office. We were led to it immediately and could even feel darkness attached to it. We prayed over it, repenting for any sin that had been committed on the desk, especially ungodly oaths or legal documents. After praying, we all felt the darkness leave, and a peace from the Lord came.

As you clear each room, you can anoint the room as you go. Then, when the whole house has been anointed, you go on to burn the objects or destroy them. If an object won't burn, you can demolish it by breaking it up with a hammer or saw, or any way that will make it unrecognizable and unusable.

We have learned that when someone puts a curse on something, sometimes the curse comes upon the person who breaks the curse. So we pray Psalm 91 over ourselves as we are burning or destroying the items that we have collected.

Whoever dwells in the shelter of the Most High will rest in the shadow of the Almighty. I will say of the Lord, "He is my refuge and my fortress, my God, in whom I trust.

Surely he will save us from the fowler's snare and from the deadly pestilence. He will cover us with his feathers, and under his wings we will find refuge; his faithfulness will be our shield and rampart.

We will not fear the terror of night, nor the arrow that flies by day, nor the pestilence that stalks in the darkness, nor the plague that destroys at midday.

A thousand may fall at our side, ten thousand at our right hand, but it will not come near us. We will only observe with our eyes and see the punishment of the wicked.

We say, "The Lord is our refuge, and we make the Most High our dwelling, no harm will overtake us, no disaster will come near our tent. For he will command his angels concerning us to guard us in all our ways; they will lift us up in their hands, so that we will not strike our foot against a stone We will tread on the lion and the cobra; we will trample the great lion and the serpent.

"Because he loves me," says the Lord, "I will rescue him; I will protect him, for he acknowledges my name, He will call on me, and I will answer him; I will be with him in trouble, I will deliver him and honor him. With long life I will satisfy him and show him my salvation." ~ Psalm 91 NIV

We then command any demons that had come with the curse to leave. We thank the Lord that there would be no repercussions upon any of us as we destroyed the items.

Anointing the outside of your home

After you have anointed the inside of your home, and burned or destroyed any objects, you then anoint the outside doors.

As you walk around anointing all of the outside doors, you can say this prayer.

Thank You Jesus for opening the eyes of our understanding, and blessing us with the gift of wisdom and discernment as we have walked through this house. Your Word says in Proverbs.

24:3, through wisdom a house is built and by understanding it is established.

We ask that if we have missed anything in this home that needs to be removed, You will bring this to___ (owners or renters) attention so we can pray over it. We thank You for the blood that gives believers the legal spiritual authority to stand in the gap on behalf of sin.

We are repenting on behalf of sin and claiming forgiveness for it in Your name. We thank You that you have given us the power of attorney to use Your name and Your blood to revoke curses and command the enemy to leave these premises.

We now apply the doorposts with the olive oil with the hyssop and the symbolic blood of the Your sacrifice that paid the price for every sin that has been committed in this home from its beginning.

As we do this, we are rehearsing what You commanded us to do in Exodus 12. You say as we do this, throughout the generations the death angel will see this symbol of covenant upon our doorposts and pass over our homes.

Thank You for Your blood that has the authority to forgive sin and cleanse this home and make it as new before You. We ask for Your presence to fill this home in a tangible way. We decree that Your purposes for this home will be fulfilled. We understand that unless You build the house, we labor in vain. (Psalm 127:1)

Thank You for keeping our home safe and that You never slumber or sleep. (Psalm 121:4) You say that there is a curse in the house of the wicked, but you will bless the habitation of the just. (Proverbs 3:33)

Thank You that the wicked shall be overthrown, but the house of the righteous shall stand. (Proverbs 12:7)

As we complete the dedication and covenanting of our home, we can pray the same prayer that David did:

I will sing of mercy and loving kindness and justice; to You, O Lord will I sing. I will behave myself wisely and give heed to the blameless way. O when will you come to me? I will walk within my house in my integrity and with a blameless heart. I will set no base or wicked thing before my eyes. I hate the work of them who turn aside (from the right path) it will not grasp hold of me. (Psalm 101:1-3 AMP)

I ask that You will help us as we set our will to behave ourselves wisely, in a way that will be pleasing to You, so that we can walk within this home with a perfect heart. Amen.

Hosting the Lord's Presence in your home

Our goal as believers is to please the Lord, not only with our lives, but also our homes, for they are an outward reflection of who we are. We should endeavor to create a space where those who come into our home will encounter the Lord. They will feel the peace and experience the joy and harmony of those who live together in the home. If you work in a worldly workplace, there is no doubt there is a need for peace and harmony.

It is important to have some way of honoring Jesus in your home that others can see. People who come into your home collect information about you without realizing it. If your home speaks of faith in Jesus, you will find that people, who may not be believers, will quickly pick up how they should act from the appearance of your home. If you have items in your home that point to Jesus, and it is their time for salvation or healing in some area, it could open up a conversation that leads to prayer. The testimony of your home can be used by the Lord to change lives. I have heard it said; "Is there enough evidence in your home to convict you of being a Christian?" That evidence may be a picture that points to Jesus in some way.

There will be those who think this isn't necessary. I do know that when light comes in to darkness, the darkness flees. Even if a person doesn't have visible proof (such as a picture hanging on their wall), they may have Christian music they play or Christian DVDs they watch, that contributes to hosting the presence of the Lord.

The Lord loves to hear worship and praise music and His Word being quoted aloud. The angels love it too, according to the Bible. As I said before, the angels will come to listen, then go forth to perform the Word that is spoken.

Psalm 103:20 says, *Bless the Lord, you His angels, Who excel in strength, who do His Word, Heeding the voice of his Word.*

"When an unclean spirit goes out of a man, he goes through dry places, seeking rest, and finds none. Then he says, 'I will return to my house from which I came.'

~ Matthew 12:43

Chapter 12

Keeping Your Home Demon Free

The enemy won't like being evicted from what he considers his home. Stay alert! He will wait a little while and try to sneak back in.

The following scripture is speaking of a man who has been delivered from demons, but it will also apply to our homes after they are cleansed.

> *"When an unclean spirit goes out of a man, he goes through dry places, seeking rest, and finds none. Then he says, 'I will return to my house from which I came.' And when he comes, he finds it empty, swept, and put in order. Then he goes and takes with him seven other spirits more wicked than himself, and they enter and dwell there; and the last state of that man is worse than the first. So shall it also be with this wicked generation."* ~ Matthew 12:43-45

This scripture is speaking of spiritual maintenance. As we cleanse and anoint our homes, we must be vigilant to keep them not only swept clean of demonic influence, but also to fill them with the presence of the Lord. We can do this with the items we use to decorate our homes, by playing Christian music, and by praying the Word of God aloud. Doing so will fill your home with angels.

When the demons return to your home to see if there is an open door for them to move back in, they will quickly figure out they aren't welcome. When you tell them there is no vacancy because the space they used to inhabit is now filled with the Lord, they have to go. Their return visit is nothing to be fearful of; the demons are just doing their job. Ours is to make sure they fail in their mission.

In Conclusion

I hope that you will be encouraged by the scriptures and the testimonies that you have read in this book, and you will be inspired to spiritually cleanse your own home, apartment or office.

You may discover that the enemy has found some hidden entrance that has given him a legal means of coming onto your land and into your home and has caused negative effects to influence those who live there.

Even though this book focuses on your home, it is just as important to spiritually cleanse your land, to bring it under the protection of covenant that you, as a believer, have with the Lord.

If you have questions about how to perform this covenant ceremony with your land, you can read about it in the book; From Gods Hands To Your Land. You can learn more about it and purchase it on our website www.gloriouscreations.net

This book wouldn't be complete without this last scripture.

Now therefore, let it please You to bless the house of Your servant, that it may continue before You forever; for You, O Lord God, have spoken it, and with Your blessing let the house of Your servant be blessed forever.
~ *2 Samuel 7:29*

Appendix

The Mezuzah is affixed to your doorpost as follows.

Roll the scroll so the text is on the inside.

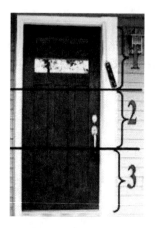

Place the Mezuzah on the upper third part of the right-hand doorpost as you enter from outside (about eye level).

Slant the Mezuzah inward so that the top of the Mezuzah is inclined towards the door and the bottom towards outside.

Fasten the Mezuzah case at the top and bottom. A blessing is offered at the time of placing the Mezuzah. '

Blessed are you, O Lord our God, ruler of the universe, who has sanctified us by your commandments and has commanded us to affix the Mezuzah.

ABOUT THE AUTHOR

 Jeanette is in active ministry. In 1997, she and her husband, Bud, founded and are the co-owners of Glorious Creations. Glorious Creations is a Worship and Praise adornment company. Jeanette is ordained as a minister through Gospel Crusade and has been in full time ministry since 1998.

She is a member of Aglow International and is an Intercessor for Southwest Michigan under the leadership of Apostle Barbara Yoder, Leader of the Breakthrough Apostolic Ministries Network, and Apostle Doug Carr, Regional Director for the Network. She is a member of Hartland Apostolic Network in Michigan (HAPN).

Books by Jeanette Strauss

Heavenly Impact -- Symbolic Praise, Worship, and Intercession —On Earth As It Is In Heaven

Impacto Divino

Heavenly Impact Teachers Manual

Heavenly Impact Student Workbook

From the Courtroom of Heaven—To the Throne Room of Grace and Mercy

From the Courtroom of Heaven — To the Throne of Grace and Mercy – Prayers and Petitions Book

From God's Hands To Your Land — Blessings!

De las Manos de Dios a Tu Tierra

These books, as well as anointing oils, kits to help you when redeeming your land, mezuzahs, and many worship adornments are available at www.gloriouscreations.net or by calling 517-639-4395

Symbolic Praise Worship & Intercession DVD
"On Earth As It is in heaven"
Volume 1

This teaching/demonstrational DVD presents a scriptural foundation, revealing the impact created in the spiritual realm when these symbolic tools are used: Tabrets, Flags, Streamers, and Veils, symbolic vocabulary of movement for each instrument shown. Many have used this DVD. to introduce their pastors to this type of praise and worship. We have received many reports back from teams of Intercessors from all over the country who say the Lord has showed up in so many supernatural ways since they began to worship with purpose with the instruments shown in the DVD, applying the scriptural information given in the teaching. 120 minutes. ISBN#0-9770180-0-8 $18.50

SYMBOLIC PRAISE WORSHIP & INTERCESSION DVD
"On Earth As It Is In Heaven"
Volume 2

This DVD explores and explains the ancient history and modern application of these four worship adornment, the shofar, the prayer shawl, rods of God, and Threshing Floor prayer mat, and their strategic purpose according to Scripture. Includes Biblical references concerning how these instruments reveal that our actions here on earth affects actions in heaven. Two hours of exciting teaching/ demonstration. ISBN# 0-9770180-1-6. $18.50

Heavenly Impact

Symbolic Praise, Worship, and Intercession
"On Earth As It Is In Heaven"

This book is a 'must read' for those seeking a Biblical foundation for the use of symbolic tools of praise, worship and intercession. This information presents clear guidelines concerning their proper place and use.

Explore the Possibilities!

Heavenly Impact guides you through Bible history and explains the relevance of worship adornment as it identifies strategic value to worship. Scripture references reveal that our actions on earth truly do have a "Heavenly Impact". Tools covered: flags, billows, Mat-teh', shofar, streamers, tabrets, and veils, vocabulary of movement and Biblical color symbolism. $14.00

Also available is a 12-week course, with both a *Teachers Manual and a Student Workbook*. This is an easy to understand course that teaches the principles covered in the *Heavenly Impact* book. At the end of each chapter are prophetic exercises and activations, discussion topics, and a biblical color chart. Can be purchased as a set with the *Heavenly Impact* book, or individually.

From God's Hands To Your Land—
Blessings

The Bible establishes the spiritual relationship between God and His land. The Lord desires to pour out His blessings on your land, but scripture says that His blessings can be blocked.

The Lord, as the Owner of the original title deed of all real estate, gave us the responsibility to subdue and take dominion over the land. Included in this book are step-by-step instructions for the Restoration Ceremony, with prayers and decrees to recite as you reconcile and redeem your land that will ensure that His blessings will flow freely on your land with no hindrances. Also available in Spanish. $10.00

Bless Your Land
KIT

This kit contains the items you will need for the Restoration Ceremony.

It contains: 1 copy of the book, *From God's Hands to Your Land*, 4 communion cups with wafers, milk, honey, harvest seeds, consecration oil, a Title Deed. $20.00

From the Courtroom of Heaven
to the Throne Room of Grace and Mercy

As a born-again Christian, I had never given the Courtroom of Heaven a thought. Then, in answer to our prayer for our backslidden daughter, the Lord gave me a dream. The dream contained the proper protocol to use in the Courtroom of Heaven on her behalf. As a result, she was set free and restored.

This book includes the dream and the strategy the Lord revealed. You can use this same protocol and win your own petitions in the Courtroom of Heaven. Show up where the accuser of the brethren does not expect, and win your case! $14.00

Courtroom Prayers and Petitions Book

This is a companion to the book " *From the Courtroom of Heaven to the Throne of Grace and Mercy.*" Includes prayers for presenting a petition, preparing for your court appointment, cleansing prayer for yourself, The breaking of a generational bloodline curse, marriage, separation/divorce, healing of the brokenhearted , future spouse;. healing of sickness, deliverance from addictions, depression/ mental confusion, business success; destiny-direction for life including Job or geographical location shift, prayer for the unsaved or backslidden. $13.00